CAN I JUST TAKE A NAP?

By Ron Rauss

Illustrated by Rob Shepperson

A Paula Wiseman Book
Simon & Schuster Books for Young Readers
NEW YORK   LONDON   TORONTO   SYDNEY   NEW DELHI

To Aiden and Erica, the two best things that ever happened to me
All my love—R. R.

For Maia and Luna—R. S.

ACKNOWLEDGMENTS
The author would like to say a heartfelt thank-you to
everyone involved with the Cheerios® New Author Contest
and to his wonderful family and friends.

SIMON & SCHUSTER BOOKS FOR YOUNG READERS
An imprint of Simon & Schuster Children's Publishing Division
1230 Avenue of the Americas, New York, New York 10020
Text copyright © 2012 by Ron Rauss • Illustrations copyright © 2012 by Rob Shepperson
SIMON & SCHUSTER BOOKS FOR YOUNG READERS is a trademark of Simon & Schuster, Inc.
For information about special discounts for bulk purchases, please contact
Simon & Schuster Special Sales at 1-866-506-1949 or business@simonandschuster.com.
The Simon & Schuster Speakers Bureau can bring authors to your live event.
For more information or to book an event, contact the Simon & Schuster Speakers Bureau at 1-866-248-3049
or visit our website at www.simonspeakers.com.
Book design by Chloë Foglia • The text for this book is set in Skizzors.
The illustrations for this book are rendered in pen and ink with watercolor.
Manufactured in China • 0312 SCP
2 4 6 8 10 9 7 5 3 1
Library of Congress Cataloging-in-Publication Data
Rauss, Ron.
Can I just take a nap? / Ron Rauss ; illustrated by Rob Shepperson.
p. cm.
"A Paula Wiseman Book."
Summary: Surrounded by hubbub and noise, a little boy
longs for someplace quiet where he can take a nap.
ISBN 978-1-4424-3497-4 (hardcover : alk. paper)
[1. Stories in rhyme. 2. Noise—Fiction.] I. Shepperson, Rob, ill. II. Title.
PZ8.3.R2324Can 2012
[E]—dc23
2011019438
ISBN 978-1-4424-3498-1 (eBook)

first
edition

Aiden McDoodle was tired of noise.
He was tired of TV, he was tired of toys.

He was tired of knocking, he was tired of ringing.
He couldn't take any more of the little birds' singing.

There was too much noise inside and too much noise out.
There was panting and pawing from his trusty dog, Scout.

There were radios blaring and cars that would beep.
Aiden McDoodle just wanted some sleep.

He tried closing the doors, he tried covering his head.
He tried upstairs and downstairs, he tried under the bed.

He tried the backyard, the library, and even the park.
But at each place he tried, there was a buzz or a bark.

The backyard was crawling with bugs big and small.
They chirped when they heard his brother yell,

"CANNONBALL!"

In the library the whispers built up to a riot,
until the librarian stepped in and shouted out,

"QUIET!"

The park roared with laughter
as players cheered for their team.
Then a stampede broke out
when someone hollered,

"ICE CREAM!"

Noise came from all over, from up high and down low.
It started out faint but then continued to grow.

There was rocking and rolling and bouncing and bumping,
clanging and banging and tapping and thumping.

Aiden McDoodle was hanging on by a thread.
All that he wanted was his warm, comfy bed.

He didn't want to yell; it wasn't like him to bellow.
But Aiden McDoodle was one tired fellow.

He had tried to be patient, but they left him no choice.
So Aiden shouted out at the top of his voice,

"I don't mean to be rude,
but I'm ready to snap!
Can you all please be quiet
so I can just take a nap?"

He had yelled it so loudly, it was heard sea to sea,
from the deepest of valleys to the tallest of trees.

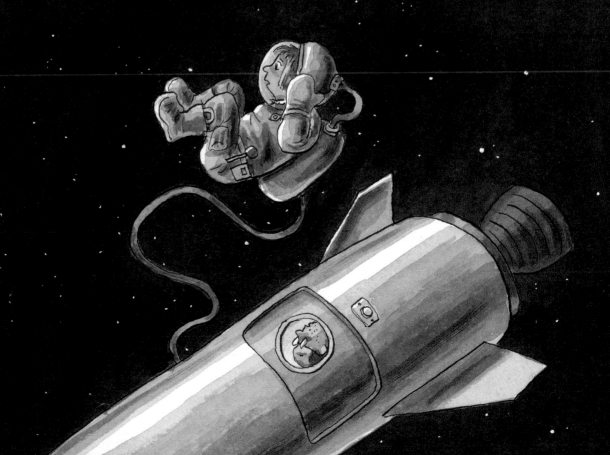

Then all of a sudden everything stopped.
Nothing buzzed, blared, or beeped; not a single thing popped.

Not a squirt or a squeal; not a squeak from a mouse.
Aiden was so happy, he ran straight for his house.

He rushed up the stairs and jumped right into bed.
He fluffed up his pillow and then he laid down his head.

The noisemakers were impatient; they couldn't keep this up long,
without someone talking or tweeting or singing a song.

And just as they couldn't take the silence much more . . .

ZZZZZZZZZZZZZZ...

Aiden McDoodle started to

s n o r e .

Sweet dreams.